The Stories of Sister Sarah

Whispers of the Dead

David Clark

1

"Good morning Ralph, Kenneth," Sister Sarah greeted the two young filmmakers who had arrived to hear yet another story from her life. Today they met Sarah in the convent's library, Kenneth's idea. After their first visit, Mother Francine gave them a quick tour of the grounds as they were leaving. The old tall wooden bookcases spoke to Kenneth the minute he saw them. The request was immediate, as was the acceptance.

They had planned to get there early and be setup when Sarah Meyer arrived, that was not the case. She was already there, waiting on them with her two ever-present escorts.

"Morning, Sister. I hope you slept well," Ralph returned the greeting and looked around the room.

Sarah saw this and knew exactly what he was looking for. "My brother will be along shortly. He is an early riser, but remember, this is early by a few hours, even for him." She walked around the room while her escorts stayed equidistant on opposite sides of the room. Her movements were graceful and smooth, not showing any effects of her many years. She turned and looked back at the library and said, "Kenneth, why don't you setup here. I can sit on that side of the table, and Ralph on the other, opposite me. The books will be a great backdrop, don't you think?"

Kenneth looked at where she stood and then back at the library, but only nodded in agreement.

"Come take a look?", she requested, and motioned for him to join her on that spot.

His wide-eyed reaction and gulp drew a smirk from Sarah. "Oh, come now. I am just an old woman. I can't hurt you, and you don't need to worry about him. Come on," she prodded.

After a few reluctant steps, Kenneth joined her on the spot. With a motherly touch, she gripped and turned his shoulders so he would see what she saw. Her hand pointed out the table and how the bookcase would frame the image of both of them talking quite well. He must have agreed since he retrieved the tripod and set it right there before starting to run the wires for sound, another old-fashioned touch. Like Ralph and his written notes, they also liked the sound and reliability of the older equipment. Similar to her father and Louis Tillingsly listening to old records from their youth, while she and Jacob rolled their eyes and pushed Bluetooth earphones in their ears to block out the noise. Her father swore the records sounded better than any digital copy. A point that Sarah didn't argue with at the time, but in later years she heard a few records and had to agree there was a richness and fullness that the digital copies couldn't produce.

The library was quiet, as libraries often are and should be. The occasional sound of a cord dragging across the cobblestone floor echoed through the chamber. Kenneth's tripod let out a squeak while he twisted the collar to tighten the neck to lock it in place. He paused at how loud it sounded and the four sets of eyes that focused on him. Resuming slower this time.

"Sorry I am late," Jacob said as he entered the door with a creak.

"Not a problem, lazy boy," Sarah said with a smirk that reminded everyone that deep inside all of us are the children that still will poke fun at a sibling.

When he entered, Kenneth was almost finished setting up and Ralph and Sarah had taken their spots. Sarah spotted her brother looking around the library for where he might sit. She patted the seat next to her. "It's all right, I hope?" she asked Ralph.

"Of course, Sister. Whatever makes you most comfortable."

Sarah smiled and reached over with her left hand and slid the chair out for Jacob. With no hesitation, he walked to the chair, took off his overcoat, placed it over the back of the chair, and had a seat.

"Shall we?", she asked.

Ralph looked at Kenneth, who said, "Ready." A red light turned on at the front of the camera aimed at the three at the table. The lens turned ever so slowly to bring them into focus. "All yours, Ralph."

"Sister Sarah, thank you for seeing us again."

"My pleasure," she said.

"During our last discussion, you told us about your visit to the island of Povelgia. That was your first time out with Father Lucian on, what the Vatican called in their book, a mission to restore faith."

Sarah giggled at the term, an uncontrollable response that she caught before it continued for any prolonged period. Some might consider it disrespectful. A part of her did, but it was something she couldn't help. The Church had gone far enough to acknowledge the existing of ghosts and the keepers, but still danced around admitting to, or using the term that best described what they really did, exorcisms.

"What I would like to discuss today is something that occurred seven years later."

"You want to talk about St. Augustine," she interrupted.

"Yes, how did you guess?", asked Ralph with a dazed look on his face.

"I have been on over one hundred missions," she managed to say without a laugh, "most were rather non-descript, so I am sure you are not here to talk about those. There are several that are more interesting. St Augustine was one of them."

"Yes, it was very interesting. It was the first time you worked with your Father, but more interesting, the first recorded interaction between the Vatican and law enforcement."

"And solved three murders," Sarah proudly added.

"Yes, wait. Three?", Ralph asked. Surprise was written all over his face. Kenneth looked up from behind the camera. Jacob sat back in his chair and crossed his arms.

"You didn't know about that, did you? Not all the details were in what the Vatican wrote. There are a few that neither myself, nor Father Lucian, told them. It wasn't necessary. See, even back then, I knew the day would come when the secrets would be let out, and some secrets need to be protected."

Ralph motioned to Kenneth, who turned stopped recording. "Sister, are you ready to tell those secrets now?"

Jacob leaned forward, bracing his forearms on the table as he turned to look at his sister. A palpable tension flooded the room. One that Sarah cut, not with a knife, but with her signature amused laugh that she had had since she was a little girl.

"In a way. I can tell you the story without exposing anything that should be protected. If that is all right?" She looked at Ralph for agreement, but the look was a grandmotherly one that conveyed she wasn't really asking for an agreement, she was telling.

"Of course." Ralph waved Kenneth back behind the camera and when the red light came on he continued, "Sister, tell us about St. Augustine."

2

Sister Sarah stood over a sink with her sleeves rolled up to her elbows and soap suds halfway up her forearms. In front of her, enough baking trays to bake bread for an entire army sat soaking. It was not an army the Sisters of San Francesco were feeding; it was the town. Twice a week, every week, they spent the morning baking bread before heading into town to deliver it to the elderly, sick, and needy.

When Sarah had first arrived, she'd confined herself to the baking side of this task, and of course the cleaning, which made the scene before her a common one. It took four years before she finally trusted herself enough to venture into town.

During their visits, the Sisters delivered nourishment for both the body and the soul. Her first visit to town was also the first time Sarah had delivered a prayer to someone other than herself. It was something she'd expected to feel odd, and it did, at first. The way the kind eyes of the older women had looked at her from below her curly locks of silver hair had made Sarah hesitate. The woman expected the touch and word from the divine, and Sarah felt anything but either. She felt tainted and unworthy to deliver such words and comfort. Then Sarah remembered how those words made her feel and started. The words flowed out of her with meaning and feeling, just like they did when she said them for herself. It felt natural. Sarah took the oath two years before, but she hadn't performed any public duties before that moment. Doing that one task made her feel whole.

Sarah's waterlogged hands resembled those of an older woman, hands like Mother Demiana, she thought. There was no disrespect, just something she noticed as she looked at her own after handing the last of the baking pans to Sister Francine. It was nearly noon, and they both, along with Sarah's ever present escort, had been in the convent's kitchen since just after six in the morning. Behind them, Sister's Maria and Nanette were bundling the bread in towels and baskets for the afternoon's delivery. A simple knock on the door signaled a visitor that was not just one of the other sisters. They wouldn't have knocked, and instead would have entered to take care of whatever task had brought them to the kitchen.

Each stopped what they were doing and directed their attention to the door. Father Lucian entered, holding his wide-brimmed black hat against his chest.

"Father, it is great to see you," beamed Sarah. She dried her hands and proceeded over to give him a hug.

The rest of the sisters stayed where they were and greeted him with a "Good day, Father."

"Its good to see you, Sarah. Baking, I see."

"Yes, Father. It is Thursday," she said. "What brings this visit?"

"Let's talk somewhere else. I need your help, if you are up to it."

There was a murmur in the background, and Sarah looked around to see her sisters smiling and giggling. Sarah's exploits over the last six years had made her a celebrity, not something she wanted, yet not something that had gotten out of control. To date, Sarah had assisted Father Lucian in twenty-seven cases, solving twenty seven paranormal mysteries and disturbances. Some had even called her a real-life version of the Father Dowling, but she paid it no attention. The outings were what she viewed as her penance for what she'd caused and what she was. Not to mention, she quite enjoyed them. There was a thrill of discovery in each one. The discovery of something within herself and, of course, the truth. "Of course, Father. Lead the way." She hung up her dish towel and followed him out, her escorts in tow. Inside, she knew the trip she had so looked forward to was now not in her future.

"What is it Father?", she asked as they walked side by side down the narrow hallway and out to the central courtyard. He sat on the simple wooden bench. Sarah wanted to join him, but instead picked the bench across the circular bird bath from him, to ensure there was room for the others. She didn't have any idea how long they would be there and had always considered them in such matters.

The midday sun was high in the sky and didn't cast many shadows. Those it did were short. It felt warm and rejuvenating on her face. Father Lucian's face wasn't in the sun like hers was. The setting, and the deep distress she felt inside of him, accentuated the lines and creases of his features. She wasn't telepathic or empathic. She could only feel those not living, but in her years of service she had developed an educated sense that told her when someone was troubled. Her gaze studied him through the tumbling water that bubbled up in the fountain on top of the birdbath. Two swallows were taking full advantage of the refreshing drink.

"There has been an incident," he said, and then stopped.

"Father, there is always an incident," she started and then she caught herself. Could something have happened to someone she knew? That was always a fear, and being so far away, she may not receive word directly. Father Lucian would be the obvious choice to deliver such news.

"Father, is everyone all right?", she asked, a touch of a tremble in her voice, her hand raced to her heart.

"Yes, they are all fine. In fact, they may be helping with this," he said with a distant stare before righting himself and adjusting his posture to sit up straight and look right at her. "We have a job to do, but this one is different, I am afraid. There has been a murder and, well, to my own surprise, the authorities are pointing to something from the unnatural world and asked for help. Of course, you know who that falls to." He held his arms out wide and then pointed to himself and across to her. "Now, I have seen a great many things tied to death. Possessions, and even exorcisms that have gone wrong, but this is something new for both of us. This victim, based on everything that they have presented me, was not possessed, or even aware of the paranormal world. They were targeted and murdered in, if you can believe it, cold blood. No motivation, that anyone can find."

"Father, this would have to be a demon. A normal spirit couldn't," she stopped and then corrected herself, "wouldn't do anything like this. They are tied to events and other spirits. Unless..."

"There is a connection," Father Lucian interrupted. A smile crossed his face, which Sarah had to assume was a show of his approval for how far she had come. "That is what they want us to find out. To determine if it really was a spirit or demon that did it and find the connection. Remember, even if it is a demon, there has to be a purpose. They don't just kill for the fun of it. Everything has a purpose."

"That is true. So when are we going?"

"Well. We need to leave now. The jet is waiting for us as we speak."

"Oh," she sprang up. "Then I must get my things. Where are we going?" Sarah started for the hallway that led back to her room.

"St. Augustine, in Florida."

Sarah stopped in her tracks and turned. "St. Augustine?"

"Yes, know it?"

"I do. I went there," she started, and then thought better of the explanation. Being a Sister of the cloth made it seem inappropriate to talk about that spring break trip her and Charlotte had taken to Daytona when they were twenty. "I visited there once."

"Well, you are about to visit again, because that is where we are going." Father Lucian pushed up from his bench. "My things are already in the SUV, and the driver is waiting. Speaking of waiting, your father and Father Murray will be there when we arrive. They are both on their way now to do some pre-work on the area, and to calm the local authorities."

"And Jacob?", she asked, with hope in her heart.

"I am afraid not, dear. He is staying home to tend to the farm and things there in Miller's Crossing."

As disappointed as she felt at hearing Jacob wouldn't be there, her insides were all a flutter at the thought of seeing her father and Father Murray again, and she practically skipped back to her room.

3

"Dad," Sarah screamed as she ran through the doors of the Fly-By Cafe of the Northeast Florida Regional Airport. Her father stood up from the booth just in time to catch her in his arms. Her momentum shoved him backward against the table, jostling the glasses of water and two cups of coffee he and Father Murray had enjoyed as they waited for Sarah and Father Lucian to arrive. The elderly priest slipped past the two of them and stood waiting, next in line for a long-awaited embrace. Edward had visited his daughter several times, but Father Murray hadn't seen her since she left Miller's Crossing. When Sarah let go of her father, she jumped over to Father Murray. Edward continued his greeting with a hardy handshake and pat on Father Lucian's shoulder. Her two escorts remained at the door. The sight of a priest and three nuns entering the small airport cafe in this rural portion of northern Florida town drew the looks of those sitting in the booths enjoying their tuna melt or a slice of what the sign said was fresh baked apple pie. Sarah had to believe this was a first for this place.

Father Murray and Edward led them outside to the waiting van. It was white, with double doors on one side to provide access to the two bench-style seats in the back. Black lettering on the side said, Cathedral Basilica of St. Augustine Youth Ministry. Sarah looked at it, and then at her father and Father Murray, then back at the van, and another look, with a smirk, at the two men she had known for years. "I leave you guys alone for a few years, and you start stealing vans from churches."

Father Murray sniped back, "Hey, we are left without your good influence, Sister. Actually, we are just borrowing it while you are here. We needed something large enough to transport everyone."

Edward held open the back door for her, like he had when she was a child. "I wish Jacob could have been here," Sarah said as she stepped in and slid across the bench.

"He wanted to, but the harvest is coming and he had a lot to do. He is obsessed," Edward said.

"It's better than being possessed," Sarah said with a laugh. She meant it as a joke, but the stares she got from everyone, including her escorts that had slipped into the bench behind her, told her she'd failed. She felt as uncomfortable as she had that time she let some gas slip out in a quiet class room in the fifth grade. Every kid in the room had looked at her before exploding with laughter. There was no laughter this time. "I am joking, ha ha," she said, and she could swear she saw a few of them let out a long exhale before getting in the van themselves.

They drove down US 1, also called the Dixie Highway, toward the downtown area. Sarah had stopped here on the way back from Daytona and noticed how touristy the whole thing looked for a small town. Coming back these many years later, she found it hadn't really changed much. You had old homes and buildings from the Spanish colonial area, mixed in among modern gas stations and mini markets. Some of the buildings were still homes, but had been converted into bed and breakfasts. Each advertising how old they were on a brightly painted wooden sign hanging off a post or porch banister. The stores were much the same. Old homes fashioned into small clothing stores, with people in period clothing standing outside to invite you in. A contrast to the occasional modern looking office.

The closer you were to the waterfront, the more lost in time you became. Entire blocks were closed off from traffic, preserving an area much like it had been for almost four hundred years. As the traffic crept past those roads it left Sarah to wonder. A story her father found in an old diary said the first Meyers were smuggled in by the Vatican, through St. Augustine. Had they walked those roads, maybe stayed in one of the inns that still stood there. Or were they housed in the cathedral that stood behind it, by the central plaza? This was a piece of her history she appreciated.

"Detective Borrows wants to talk to us first, before we go to the museum," Father Murray told them. "He will meet as in Constitution Plaza, the site of the old historic market."

"What have you been able to find out?", asked Father Lucian.

"Well, you are in one of the oldest cities in the country. So as you would expect, there are ghost stories on every corner," said Edward.

"And ghost?", Father Lucian asked.

"Yes, there are," Sarah said. They were there, she knew it, she felt it. None close at the moment, but they were in the area.

"Oh, yes, and a sprawling ghost tour business. We even went on one last night."

"You what?", Sarah asked, exploding forward in her seat to push her head up between Father Murray and her father. "Say again?"

"Well, what your father said isn't completely true," Father Murray confessed. "We went on two."

Sarah exploded back in her seat. Laughter rolled out of her in a way it hadn't in longer than she could remember. Father Lucian appeared to share in the humorous nature of what they had both heard, and chuckled himself.

"It was research, and we had the time," her father tried to explain.

"Let me get this right. Two of the most legendary ghost hunters in the world took a ghost tour?", Sarah asked, barely able to form the words through her laughter. She watched from behind the two men and saw even Father Murray's shoulders rise and drop a few times as he laughed.

"It would seem so, but we had a point to it."

Sarah gathered herself and attempted to contain her laughter while she listened to Father Murray's explanation.

"What we were asked to look into was no unimportant matter. We wanted to find out what kind of local legends may exist that could drive the fear and speculation that a poltergeist did this. You know better than anyone, Sarah, how much some of those legends can shape opinions."

He was right, she knew. Her family was the center of most of those legends. "Okay, then, what did you find?"

"Well, there are a ton of different legends here, such as, if you look out the window at the fort, Castillo de San Marcos," Father Murray said with his best attempt at a Spanish accent. "They say at night it is not uncommon to see Spanish soldiers patrolling the wall, or a Seminole Indian jumping off the top of the south-west wall. And then, over there, see that second-floor balcony? They say you can hear the clinking of mugs as the ghosts of bootleggers that used to frequent it, around the turn of the century, sit and enjoy a drink. Everywhere you look there is a story, but none larger than the other. No central, what I would call bigfoot or ghost of St. Augustine type story, which is what I was interested in learning. It seems everyone here believes, or is open-minded, but unlike our little place, they can't really see or know for sure."

"And the museum?", Father Lucian asked.

The two men in the front shared a look between them before Edward said, "I think it would be best if you walked through it first, before you are told the story. We heard the story first, and are concerned that may have clouded our judgement."

They continued along the waterfront and turned away from the water, instead of following the traffic over the ornate Bridge of Lions, to a rectangular tree-filled plaza with several monuments, a gazebo, and a large, covered structure which was the old market.

Edward pulled into a rare empty spot and the four of them got out. Sarah paused again, enjoying the sensation of the fresh breeze coming in across the Matanzas River. They were close to the ocean, she knew that. She could see the slight change in how the sky looks over a large body of water, a reflection of the light off the water and, most of all, the smell. That familiar salt smell riding on the breeze, that you only smell around the ocean. The last time she had smelled it was on a small island in Italy.

It was sunny and warm, but not overly so. People were out walking along the sidewalks that traversed through the park. Families with small kids who would stray back and forth from the concrete to the grass. People on their lunch break, hurrying along. Couples walking hand in hand, without a care for time. Sarah found her gaze following them. Not in a longing sense. At one time in her life, she'd wanted to be one of them, but she knew now that was no longer an option. Just a dream from a life that seemed so long ago. A relationship between the three of them would never work out.

Sarah and her escorts rejoined the others in the present and followed them into the park. Father Murray and Edward led the way, and greeted a man wearing a navy blue suit, paisley tie, and a lanyard around his neck with a badge swinging from it. He was a tall, thin man, but not gangly. He had a good three inches on her father, and would have a good six or seven on her. As she approached, she heard her father handle the introductions. "Detective, this is Father Lucian, and my daughter, Sarah," Edward caught himself and then corrected it with a nod toward her, "Sister Sarah."

Sarah, never forgetting her protectors, looked behind her and introduced Sister Mary Theresa and Sister Cecilia. "They are with me," she said.

"The Vatican representatives?", he asked. His voice was as syrupy smooth as a used car salesman, with just a hint of a southern drawl that might be best heard sitting on a porch telling stories while drinking one too many. Sarah's escorts had his attention. They stood six feet behind her, praying the whole time.

"We are," Father Lucian answered sternly.

"Are they okay?", the detective asked. Pointing at the two sisters behind Sarah with a hand that held a burning cigarette.

"They are fine," Father Lucian answered.

"Okay," he said, wearily at first, then moved his focus to Father Lucian. "Father Pedro wasn't sure y'all would take us serious enough to actually send anyone." His eyes caught the two sisters again, and his head turned to look right at them over Sarah's shoulder. "Are you sure they're okay? Why are they praying? That is praying, right?" he asked with his nose crinkled up, producing several lines on the bridge between his eyes.

"Yes, detective," responded Father Lucian. "It is their order. Go on."

"I want to make myself clear. We aren't the kind of department that believes in, or searches for, things that go bump in the night, but you live around these parts long enough you hear and see things. Sometimes you have a case where nothing from the natural world makes sense. That is when those things you hear and see creep in, and the otherworldly fills in the blanks." He looked around for a minute. His foot playing with a rock in the dirt, rolling it back and forth, back and forth, creating an indentation it would fit in easily. "Heck, probably anywhere else if I tell someone I need to talk to a priest about my case, or even hint at what I was going to suggest, they would take my badge and gun and laugh their asses off as they escorted me out."

"Understood, Detective. What can you tell us?"

4

"Well Father, two weeks ago, this past Thursday, a body of a woman was found burnt in the restricted upstairs quarters of the museum. She was forty-seven-year-old Lauren Middleton, a local. She was part of the tour through the museum. Most saw her and remembered her at the beginning, and various times throughout the tour." Detective Burrows reached inside his jacket and pulled out a picture and showed the others. "As you can see, she was striking, so the sort of person people remember."

The detective was right. Lauren had striking blue eyes that seemed to jump right off the picture at Sarah while she studied it. Curly black hair framed her pleasant rosy face. Her features appeared to be the sort that couldn't frown if she tried.

"What was the source of the fire?", Father Lucian asked. Both Father Murray and Edward looked on with heavy anticipation, and Sarah wondered why.

"There was no fire. Not even the slightest hint of smoke."

Sarah now knew why her father and Father Murray had the looks they had plastered on their faces.

Father Lucian's head flinched backwards. "I don't understand," Father Lucian explained.

Sarah had been through many odd situations with Father Lucian through the years. Demons, poltergeist, lost souls, those messing with things they shouldn't, such as black magic, and a few Sarah didn't know how to characterize. Even the two-year-old that sat with him once and calmly discussed the hierarchy of demons and where they fit in it, all the while quoting "Pseudomonarchia Daemonum" the whole time. Nothing ever appeared to surprise him. In fact, he appeared to rather enjoy the debate with the two-year-old. This had him off kilter.

"Father, there was no fire. Nothing burnt, but her. Mind you, some of the exhibits in that place are old and non-replaceable. They tune the smoke detectors to go off if a person strikes a match. Nothing went off. They found her, two days after the tour. The cleaning crew found her while doing their weekly pass through the upper floor, which is off-limits to guests."

"Could she had been killed and burnt somewhere else, and then brought back?", Sarah asked, looking for a logical explanation. Their presence there hinted to her that these had been worked through, but she needed to ask and be sure. One thing Father Lucian had always reminded her during her training, don't be so quick to the conclusion that the paranormal was involved with a situation. Sometimes, many times, there was a logical explanation. It was a hard lesson for her to learn to apply, but eventually became second, well maybe third, nature.

"We considered that. That was until we watched the security footage. Cameras cover every door, window, and the entire parking lot. There is no way anyone could leave or enter that place without being on camera. She never left, and definitely wasn't snuck back in like this." Detective Burrows pulled out a second picture and passed it around. "Before you ask the next question that I imagine is in your mind, yes, those are burns."

Sarah winced and her stomach turned at the gory sight. Only her stark blue eyes remained unburnt. Everything else was charred black.

"What about the smell?", Father Lucian asked.

This question sent Sarah's stomach into another somersault. She knew exactly what Father Lucian was asking. Burnt flesh has a rather distinctive and putrid odor. It was one Sarah had become familiar with on her first mission with Father Lucian to Poveglia. Since then she had encountered it twice. Fire, and incineration, are important symbols in their world. It was seen both as a cleanser and destroyer. Set a person on fire, and you cleanse the soul. It had been used for hundreds of years, through every period of religious persecution, all the way up through the Salem witch trials. The other side believes fire to be the great destroyer, the rapture's lake of fire. Through all of her case studies, Sarah had noticed demons often used fire as a way to manipulate the living. Each had something in common with what she saw. The fire damage often disappeared, and when it didn't, only the target of their action, the person, was scarred, as if it was a blemish on their soul.

"No smell, either. Not in the building. Once we removed her from the building, the smell of burnt flesh was overwhelming in the coroner's office. By the way, his report said she was burnt from the inside out."

Sarah spied her father looking at them, smiling, as her brain worked over the details to the ultimate conclusion. There was no natural explanation.

"Suspects?", asked Father Lucian

"Well, no," Detective Burrows fumbled. He looked down at the rock he had worked over before and restarted the task. "I mean, we checked a list of her family, friends, coworkers, and exes a few dozen times." His head shot up and his eyes narrowed. They were in the shade, so that wasn't to shield from the glare as he looked around at all four of his visitors. "Look, we checked out all the normal stuff, and there was nothing. No suspects. No motive. Hell, how do you even burn someone from the inside? Is that even physically possible? We are kind of going out on a limb to bring you guys in on this, but there are no answers in our world for this, and things just line up."

"Line up with what?", Sarah asked. Her curiosity was more than piqued.

"Hold up, detective," Father Murray interrupted. "I think it would be best for them to walk around the museum and get a feel for things before they hear those details. They need to have a clear point of view."

5

After dropping off Sister Cecilia at the church, where quarters were made for each of them, they proceeded to the museum. Sister Mary Theresa would be her daytime escort, and Sister Cecilia would be responsible for Sarah at night. Having only one at the convent was a common occurrence, and only recently had she started to venture outside those protective walls with only one. Not that there wasn't someone there to help if something happened. Either Mother Demiana or Father Lucian were with her on each of those excursions, and they could more than manage her.

When they arrived at the museum, Sarah and Sister Mary Theresa marveled at the outside of it. To say the building was eclectic would be an understatement. On the outside, it appeared to be a miniature version of the old Spanish fort just down the road. Inside, it was a combination of old Spanish home and turn of the twentieth century styling. Right down to the rich usage of the colors red and yellow in the furnishings in the non-public entrance, spaces used only by the staff, and for the ghost tours. The museum itself had been closed since the incident happened, and yellow crime scene tape was still wrapped around the handles of the large doors where the general public entered.

The office entrance had remained mostly closed as well. Only opening for the local police investigating the murder, and then Father Murray and Edward the night before. Wendy Marcus was the person who opened the doors each of those times, she now opened them for a third time. Her official title was curator, but as Father Murray explained on the ride over from the plaza, it was more general manager. The museum of oddities had added nothing new in years, and the decision to do so, as well as the decision to rotate any exhibits to and from another site, could only be made by the corporate entity. Not to say she was not well versed in the history and story of the building and every exhibit. She had to be, as she served as a tour guide as well.

"Shall we start the tour?", Wendy asked. Her hands were clasped in front of her, and Sarah noticed the cherub face on the squat woman took on a serious but well-rehearsed look. She was about to start her show.

"Actually, Mrs. Marcus," Edward started, but was interrupted.

"It's Miss, and just Wendy."

"Okay, all right, Wendy. I think it would be best if they just walk around on their own first and get a sense of the place. If that is all right with you?"

"Well," she said with a bit of a huff. "I guess so." She moved aside, out of the doorway, deflated.

Father Lucian took off his wide brimmed black hat and handed it Father Murray, "Father?"

"Of course."

Then he, Sarah, and Sister Mary Theresa passed by Wendy and into the hallway that led straight into the museum. This was not like any museum Sarah had ever seen. It was case upon case of the strangest objects in the world. Skulls of deformed creatures. Beaded fertility necklaces. Paintings done on the head of a pin, which Sarah stopped and squinted through the magnified glass on the display case to see the image. The detail was unbelievable. So unbelievable she thought it might be a hoax, with the picture painted on the glass instead, but when she looked she found clear glass.

Each room opened back into a central opening that ran to the ceiling. A forty foot tall motorized Ferris-wheel, made from erector set parts, stood proudly in that space. Its cars rotated up and around slowly. One after another, over and over again. They continued, together the whole time, past a full-sized picture of a man who had body modifications performed to make him look like a lizard, and through the room dedicated to pirates, obviously themed because of the history of St. Augustine itself.

"So, I wonder what piece in this place is haunted?", Sarah asked as she studied a wall lined with burial masks.

"I doubt it is that simple," replied Father Lucian.

"Yep," agreed Sarah. She knew it wasn't, she felt it, and could tell he did, too. She walked around and studied the exhibits like a tourist, though she would argue it was part of her investigation to try to learn what they were dealing with. Father Lucian avoided the exhibits and instead kept his path to the center of each room. There was something there. That was an undeniable fact. Sarah had felt many things since she stepped off the plane. St. Augustine had ghosts to go with all of its ghost stories. That was a fact. The museum had its own story and ghost, or possibly ghosts, to go along with it.

On the third floor the feelings became stronger and wasn't just a "something", and had now manifested itself in the all too familiar pin-pricks on the back of her neck. They grew stronger the further she moved in the third floor, past an optical illusion of a woman in a shower. From one angle she was there, from the other she was gone. Sarah stopped, prompting Father Lucian to ask, "What is it?"

Sarah held up a single finger at first, and then stood dead still, listening, feeling. It was there, with them. Not on that floor with them, but close. It was above them, in the space blocked off to the general public. The floor where the victim was found.

Sarah sprinted around, the heels of her shoes thudding on the wooden floor. Each thud echoed. She was searching for something, some place. The place where the feeling was the strongest. It would be there that she could reach out and sense the most, possibly even see it, if it wanted to be seen. If it didn't, she had her way to make it.

At first, the far northeast corner seemed to give Sarah the strongest feeling, but as she moved around, she found the center of the room was equally as strong, but different. Walking back toward the first corner, Sarah felt that feeling fade, but it never went away completely. It changed, or merged, and became something, or someone, different. There were two entities. She was sure of it. One above them in the center of the room. The other above where she was now. That was the only explanation for the two spots and the two slightly different feelings she felt.

"There are two," she reported to Father Lucian, who paced from the far corner along the wall to the door and back.

"I agree. One right here, by the door, and the one you have over there."

"No," she said, confused by what he said. If there was one by the door, that would make three. She didn't come through that door that lead in from the hall, but instead entered from the neighboring room. Sarah joined him by the door, and just as he reported, there was something here. It was unmistakable, and it was strong. The tingling she felt up her neck was just on the verge of being painful, like a dozen needles jabbing in and out of her skin. There was something else, too. A darkness that appeared to drip down from the ceiling toward her. "There are three."

"What?" Father Lucian stopped his pacing and spun around toward Sarah.

"Yes, Father. One in that corner over there," she pointed to the opposite corner. "One in the center of the room, right under the light, and this one here. The others aren't as strong or dark as this one. This one is evil."

Father Lucian made long strides across the room. Each step echoed in the room. When he reached the center he paused, but only for a second. Then he continued on to the other corner, where he paused again and then spun around on his heels before marching back to Sarah in the doorway.

"I see. I can feel them, but can't feel anything specific."

"I can't either, just the malevolent intention of the one here. I am still too far away to sense any more, or to see them."

"Then we need to fix that," Father Lucian said and then headed off.

Sarah and Sister Mary Theresa followed him in and out of every room on the floor, headed for what she had to assume were the stairs to the floor above them. The building was a maze of normal rooms and others that had been reconfigured to funnel you in a certain direction and out the other end. They found themselves turned around many times, retracing their steps, before finally reaching the back stairwell they had used to come up from the floor below. The problem that now faced them was the locked door that blocked them from going any further. Father Lucian shook on the knob of the door, and Sarah noticed something. This door was not part of the original structure. Everything else in this building was old. Solid wood trim, plaster, and solid wood doors. This door was metal and rattled as he pulled on it. The surrounding walls flexed a little against the strain. They were drywall, not plaster like everything else. They had sealed this stairwell off, but why?

6

"Miss Marcus," Father Lucian called as he hurried down the hallway back toward the office.

"It's just Wendy, Father," she reminded him.

"Wendy, can you open the door to the stairs up to the top floor?"

"Oh, no can do. We are under strict orders to only open that for cleaning," she said with a hint of authority, as if to remind everyone there that she was the curator.

"Who can?", he asked. "It is imperative that we get upstairs."

"It's not part of the tour."

"This is not a tour, it's an investigation," he said.

Sarah could tell, based on her experience with Father Lucian, he was growing frustrated. His hands became more animated as he spoke, instead of staying rather docile, and the pace of his words. While he had always tried to stay level-headed, or at least give the appearance that he had, she could always tell he was frustrated when his speech sped up.

"Wendy, remember we are here at the request of Detective Burrows," Father Murray added.

"Well," she said. He voice waffled in tone to one more subdued, defeated. "I guess you are. You mustn't touch anything up there. All right?"

"Yes, agreed. We won't touch anything."

She stood there for a second, lost in thought, before she turned back toward the office. "Let me get the key."

"Sarah, what did you find?", asked Edward.

"There are three spirits up there. Father Lucian and I both felt them."

Father Murray laughed and reached into his pocket, pulling out his wallet. He reached inside with a smirk on his face, searched for a moment, and then pulled out a five-dollar bill, handing it to Edward.

"Thank you very much, Father," Edward said. He shoved the bill into the front pocket of his pants. "He thought he only felt two, but I insisted there were three," explained Edward. "One was evil."

Sarah high-fived her father, "You still have it."

Both Father Lucian and Sister Mary Theresa appeared to be rather amused by this. It added a jovial sense to the moment, but that ended just as quickly as it appeared when Wendy re-emerged holding a single key up from a ring with what had to be every key to every door known to man on it. She held the one specific key they needed between her forefinger and thumb, allowing the rest to dangle below them.

Wendy walked right past Father Lucian's outstretched hand. It was obvious she had no intention of handing the keys over to anyone else, and marched through the hallway back toward the stairs. She led the parade up each flight, one step at a time, with the keys held out in front of her as if it were a lantern lighting the way. The dangling keys jingled with each step. The sound in the cavernous stairway resembled the rattling of a chain. A sound perfectly at home in a haunted house.

The parade reached the metal door leading up to the top floor. With the key still firmly between her forefinger and thumb, and the pinkie extended on that hand for no reason Sarah could figure out, Wendy turned to face them, and reminded them with a scold, "Now, remember, touch nothing."

Father Lucian nodded, but that didn't appear to be good enough as she looked around him to the others, waiting for an agreement or nod from all, even Sister Mary Theresa.

The key slipped into the lock without resistance, and Wendy turned it. In the silence of the surroundings, the clink of the metal pin and barrel in the lock was easily audible, especially when they all slid into position, opening the lock. Wendy turned the handle and pushed the door inward. A gust of stale, foul burnt air rushed out and past Sarah, rustling her hair and her habit. Which she found odd. Nothing moved on anyone else. The curly red hair on Wendy, who stood directly in front of the door, didn't even twitch.

Wendy pulled the key out and let the door open the rest of the way inside and then reached to the wall and flicked on the lights. In front of them was an ash wooden staircase, like the others in the building. The inner wall was plaster, which matched the rest of the building.

Father Lucian stepped forward to enter, but Sarah reached forward and grabbed his elbow. He stopped and looked back at her. "Let me go. I want a chance to go up there alone."

There was no objection, which Sarah hoped was a sign of the trust he had in her. She moved forward and entered the stairs with Sister Mary Theresa behind her.

The stairs creaked as they stepped up each runner, all the way to the top, where it opened up to a long hall with rooms lining either side. It all resembled an apartment or hotel. Shadows of numbers still appeared on the doors. Sarah walked carefully down the hall, making sure she was aware of what she felt, no matter how faint. The layout of the floors below them had turned her around, messing up any reference she might've had for which room they were below when they'd sensed the spirits. She stopped in front of two doors on either side of the hall from each other. Room sixteen and room seventeen. Cold pins pressed slightly into her skin from each side, and Sarah felt two distinct entities pulling at her. They were in those rooms. Of course they can't be in the same room, she thought to herself. Which room now was the decision that she pondered.

For no particular reason, her hand reached and turned the door handle for room seventeen. It opened. Again air rushed out with the smell of burnt wood. Sarah stepped inside and let her hand search the wall beside the door for a light switch. It found one that felt foreign to her touch. It was round, not flat against the wall, with the switch in the middle. When the light came on, she saw a room that time had forgotten. Everything from the bed, with the large wooden headboard with shelves built into it, that Sarah had only seen on old re-runs of *The Brady Bunch*, to the lamps on the night stands with the large hoop shades. The heavy usages of browns, light greens, and mustard yellow in everything screamed late fifties. As she walked across the room, Sister Mary Theresa entered behind her. Sarah didn't see the spirit in the room, but it still pulled her inward further, and toward another door. She turned the handle, opening up the bathroom and there, sitting on the edge of the tub with the shower curtain pushed off to one side, was the flickering image of a woman, blonde hair pinned up shoulder length, wearing just a towel wrapped around her body. Her legs dangled in the tub full of water.

"Close the door," she asked. "Close the door or he will come."

At first Sarah didn't know who she meant, and then she remembered the dark presence she'd felt below. That could be who the woman was referencing, but if it was, she had news for her. A door would not stop him.

"Please, close the door," she wailed. Her hand trembled while holding the towel closed around her chest.

Sarah rushed back to the door that led out to the hallway and closed it to appease the woman. She then needed to spiritually close the door to protect. She still didn't know exactly what they were dealing with. Sarah motioned for Sister Mary Theresa to come closer to the bathroom door and then pulled a vial out of her pocket and sprinkled the holy water in an arc behind them and continued in through the bathroom door, around the tub and back out. This practice that she had learned a few years ago from another Keeper worked best if you did it in a circle, to help focus your abilities, and to protect you from dark elements. Since then, she had used it a few times, and not always in a perfect circle, so she had faith this would work.

"He can't hurt you now," Sarah said to the woman.

In between flickers, the woman looked fully alive to her. She had full lips, high cheekbones, and glowing skin. A woman that would be called a true beauty, and she was young. Probably not much older than Sarah herself. Her big brown eyes looked at Sarah and at Sister Mary Theresa standing in the doorway. She appeared calmer now.

"Thank you. I should have never come here." She then mumbled something that Sarah couldn't fully make out, but one word was clear, "Warden".

"What was I thinking?", she said. A hint of tears glistened down her cheeks. A hand delicately reached up to wipe the tears away. "I am not that kind of woman, mind you. Not one of those hussies that frequents hotels for this kind of thing. This was just a one-time thing. An impulse, really. A simple and stupid impulse."

Sarah approached the woman, flipped down the top on the toilet, and had a seat. The woman watched her, like she was welcoming a friend, no apprehension or fear. Instead, she sat on the edge of the tub, now using the corner of her towel to dab away the tears.

Being closer now allowed Sarah to see her in greater detail. There was a depth to her. The curve of her jawbone. The high point of her cheeks. The line her collarbone made just above the towel. Even the texture of her skin showed signs of someone who was chilled, maybe after getting out of a warm bath into the chill of the room.

Sarah felt the chill, too. A combination of the spectral image in front of her, and the draft she felt in the room. The woman continued to sob and looked at Sarah and then away, out the window behind the tub. The waning moments of daylight were melting into the night, leaving a red hue. Sarah reached over and took a tissue out of the box. A puff of dust rose up in the air and followed her hand as she handed it to the woman. Before Sarah knew what she was doing, the woman took the tissue from her and said, "Thank you."

"You have nothing to fear. The door is closed. He can't harm you now," Sarah said.

"I know. It's not that. I am just stupid. I should have never come here."

"Why is that?", Sarah asked.

"I barely know him," she said, as if talking out loud to both herself and Sarah, not wanting to answer the question.

"Who is he?"

"I met him over coffee, just today. He mentioned he had a room here and asked me to come back with him. I was so foolish," she said, staring out into space the whole time.

"It's okay. Really. We all do foolish things."

"I guess we do. We are just human, aren't we, Sister?"

"Yes, we are. Why don't you tell me your name?"

The woman started to speak, and then stopped. She sniffed the air and stood up from the tub. Fear dripped from her eyes as she ran out of the room screaming, "No!" Just then, Sarah could smell what the woman must have. It was putrid and burned her nose, like gasoline or some kind of lighter fluid. Then the hint of smoke wafted in along the ceiling, like a cloud that grew. Sarah ran out of the bathroom and into the inferno that was the outer room. She looked back at Sister Mary Theresa and was about to yell for her to run, but then noticed she was calm and showed no signs of being aware of the fire around them, or the immense heat that radiated from it.

The woman ran back into the bathroom and the door slammed behind her. Sarah attempted to open the door, but the handle wouldn't turn. Behind it, the woman screamed. The terror in her voice chilled Sarah's blood. The walls vibrated around Sarah, and the bathroom door exploded open, blowing her to the floor. She ran and found the woman lifeless below the water in the tub. A black smudge covered her throat. Sarah reached down and pulled her head up above the water. A weak gasp escaped her mouth, and she said in a wispy voice, "I didn't know he was married. I didn't know." She said it over and over while the water in the tub disappeared. Her body turned into a blackened figure and then a pile of ashes that were carried away by the smoke.

Sarah walked out into the hall and, on faith, stepped through the flames. They were all around her, but did not burn her. It also consumed the hallways and adjacent rooms. The heat was getting to Sarah, and she stood there considering seeking out the other spirit for more answers, or heading back down the stairs. A wall of flames behind her sent her moving forward to the stairs. When her foot hit the top stair, the flames were gone, but the scent of freshly burned wood and flesh remained.

7

Halfway down the stairs Sarah stated, "There was a fire up there."

Wendy Marcus answered from just outside the door, at the bottom of the stairs, "Oh, no, dear. That is what is so odd about that woman. There was no fire up there," then she stopped and looked at the others. A finger came up and met her lips as she appeared deep in thought. She went to speak, but stopped before a sound escaped her mouth. By the time Wendy spoke again, Sarah and Sister Mary Theresa had made it down the stairs, but remained just inside the doorway. "Well, there was, but that was over sixty years ago, in 1944."

"Really?" Sarah stopped two steps from the bottom. "Did it have anything to do with a woman and some guy she came here to meet, named Warden?"

Wendy let out a nervous giggle and then motioned for Sarah to come out. When Sarah didn't move, Wendy's hand movements became more exaggerated as she stared at her. She slammed the door shut and quickly relocked it as soon as Sarah and Sister Mary Theresa exited. Her waddle away from the door was hurried and agitated. She didn't wait for the others, she reached the stairs and headed back down. Sarah thought she was mumbling as she did so and ran after her.

"Miss Marcus, I mean Wendy, what is it?"

The rotund woman didn't stop and bounded down the stairs with her curls and body bouncing with each step. She descended with purpose. Sarah didn't need any special training to tell she was running from something, something disturbing and frightening. It was obvious, her mind was on one track and that track led as far away from what was up those stairs as she could get, as fast as she could go.

"Wendy?", Sarah called again, but the woman didn't even acknowledge her.

Sarah then rushed down the stairs and squeezed past her, jostling the woman slightly against the rail. On instinct, Sarah apologized as she passed. On the next landing she stopped and waited for the woman, blocking her way. Sarah looked into her eyes as she often did when counseling someone who was dealing with trauma. It was a tip that Mother Demiana had given her, that seemed to instantly open someone up. A psychological trick, she'd said. There was something about the eyes of a nun looking at you in full habit that made everything all better. Sarah had yet to see it not work, this was no exception.

"Wendy, tell me what has you so frightened, my child." Sarah asked, even though Wendy had a good fifteen years, if not twenty, on her.

"It can't be," Wendy stammered. "Please tell me you know what this place is."

"It's a museum," Sarah answered, her gaze looking into the woman's bright green eyes. They shivered with fear.

"No, dear. The man's name was not Warden. You are in the Warden. This was a hotel before it was a museum, it was called the Castle Warden Inn."

Castle Warden Inn. The name and what the woman said made sense. She didn't come back with a man name Warden. She came back to the Warden with a man. That was when Sarah knew why the woman came back, and why she seemed to regret it and feel foolish. She may have even felt embarrassed talking to a nun about following a strange man back to a hotel for a sexual rendezvous. That made sense, but what happened next didn't, so Sarah asked, "Was there a fire in the hotel?"

"Oh dear, oh dear," the woman stammered and worked her way past Sarah, onto the landing. She didn't go down the next flight of stairs. Instead, Wendy searched out the closest chair she could find and had a seat. Her head buried itself in her hands. "So, you guys really can talk to ghosts?", she asked, her voice muffled and weary.

Sarah knelt down in front of Wendy and placed her hands on Wendy's knees, and with a calm and soothing voice she said, "Yes. Father Lucian, Father Murray, my father, and I can see and speak to ghosts. We can do more, too. We help people that are troubled by spirits, and help those spirits find peace. They have asked us to look into what happened." Sarah felt it was important to leave out the battles with demonic entities they often found themselves involved in, to keep everything feeling as peaceful as possible. "Now, what can you tell us?"

Wendy's head emerged from her hands. Her face was flushed, and she took a few deep breaths as she sat up. "Now, I don't believe in such stuff, but in a place like this you hear and feel things. We have all smelled smoke at various times and just learned to ignore it as one of the oddities in the history of this *odditorium*. Some of the other workers have said they have heard the voices of one of the women wailing about following him back here, and how stupid she'd been." Wendy stopped and just shook her head, "I always just chalked it up to the stories of this place playing with their mind. Yes, there was a fire here. That is a fact, and the story behind this place. This building was originally the Warden Castle Inn. It was built in the 1880s by William G Warden as a mansion for his large family. They lived in it until 1926, and it sat vacant until 1941, when it was sold to Marjorie Rawlings and her husband, you know, the woman who wrote the book "The Yearling" from over in Crosscreek. They turned and made it a really nice hotel, adding some of the amenities the Warden missed. She started inviting people she met down, and it took off. Then, in 1944, it all came crashing down. There was a fire in the upper floor that killed two women. One a Bette Nevi Richeson, of St. Augustine, the other was Ruth Pickering, from Savannah." Wendy stopped again and looked at Sarah with a light behind her eyes.

"You know, we have a pamphlet downstairs with their pictures on it, if you would like to see them."

"I would," Sarah said.

Wendy led them down to the office while she recounted the rest of the story. "Now, there are two versions of the story, and no one knows the truth. One version has it that a mysterious Mr. X killed both women and set the fire to cover it up. The problem is, other than the fire, the police found no other cause of death. Not to say the 1940s police, in a small town like this, had a lot of experience in investigating mysterious deaths."

She walked down the hall, back to the office, telling the story the whole way. Even as her voice faded into the distance, and behind walls in the small office, to retrieve the various stacks of pamphlets that would normally be stacked out in holders on a business day, for guests to take and read through as they toured the property. She started flipping through the stacks. "The other version is a little more salacious. See, Mrs. Rawlings was a little bit of a unique person, and folks say you never knew which person you were going to get. She spent a lot of time up north and elsewhere, away from her then husband, Norton Baskin. He ran the hotel and was known for his all-night poker games, and other exploits, to keep him entertained while she was away. Some say he had rooms on the upper floor reserved for women he would invite up. As you can imagine, she might not approve if she arrived home and found some 'special guests' staying. Wait.... here," she said and shoved a red folded pamphlet at Sarah. On the cover were two old black and white pictures. One was the woman Sarah had spent a few minutes talking to before the floor erupted ablaze. The second was the spitting image of their victim. "The truth behind the mystery was never solved, and it was chalked up to an electrical fire in the hotel. After that, it sat empty for a while before Ripley's bought it."

It wasn't the picture of the woman she had talked to that drew Sarah's attention to the pamphlet. It was the second picture just below it that caused her to quickly pass it around to the others, pointing to it as she handed it to them. The woman, a raven-haired beauty with striking blue eyes, had an uncomfortable resemblance to one Lauren Middleton. The two could be twins, separated by a century.

8

"Could it be that simple?", Father Murray asked from the back of the group.

"It could, very easily. I have seen it a few times," said Father Lucian.

"The Moors in Somerset?", asked Sarah.

Father Lucian merely nodded in agreement.

Wendy looked at the group as though she was a tourist in another country, watching the locals talk, without understanding the language. Her gaze watched everything, but her ears were just waiting to hear her name.

"Three years back, I think, Father Lucian and I assisted another Keeper on a case in Exmoor National Park, in Somerset. There was a spirit that was attacking hikers that were out exploring the moor. If you have ever thought about exploring a moor, don't. They look like beautiful prairies and meadows from a long way off, but they're full of thatch, holes of mud, and everything else that makes hiking in one unpleasant."

"Sarah," Father Lucian prompted.

"Oh, sorry," said Sarah with a quick roll of her eyes. "Anyways. There had been more than three dozen mysterious attacks in this National Park, all in the same general area. The location was not the only coincidence. They were all female. All hiking alone, and all mid-twenties, blonde, medium build, with brown eyes. Not a brunette in the bunch. It took a while to research local legend and deaths in the area, and we found one. A man, Donald Ward, from the late nineteenth century, who died in the moor. See, he went hunting in the moor with his dogs after he found out his wife was having an affair with another man in town. The dogs returned, but he never did. They searched the moor for two days and never found him. Some speculated he didn't go hunting at all. They believe he went out there to commit suicide, out where the moor would absorb his body. Whatever the cause of death, suicide, or something more natural, I have no doubt that place would consume the body in a way it would never be found. You can probably guess what his wife looked like. She was a mid-twenties blonde, with brown eyes."

"The trouble with Mr. Ward," Father Lucian interrupted, as he moved to the front of the group. "He never showed himself to anyone that didn't resemble her. So, as you can imagine, no matter how many times John went out there, he never saw him. Neither would we, if Sarah hadn't found a way to flush him out."

Edward looked at his daughter with one of grave concern and worry. The kind of worry that weighed your soul down. "You didn't let it..."

Before Edward was able to complete the sentence Sarah shook her head no and then directed her father's attention to her attending escort, Sister Mary Theresa. Who knew all eyes in the room had moved to her, but she kept praying the whole time through the slight smirk on her face, under her blonde hair and brown eyes. Sarah had to use her as bait to call him out. Once he was out, she was able to feel his presence and make contact. He wasn't a demon, just someone with a great deal of pain that was taking it out on who he thought was his wife. This was probably something similar, but who was the attacker? And why?

"I don't get it," Wendy said.

The entire group turned to look at the puzzled expression on her face. She stood there, slack-jawed, and looked back and forth at each of them. Sarah was the only one who stepped forward, bringing with her the pamphlet. Standing beside her, Sarah handed Wendy the pamphlet and pulled her attention to the second picture. Sarah waited for the light to go on, and when it didn't, she applied a little pressure to the switch with a question, "Recognize the picture?"

"Of course. The first picture is Bette Robertson, and the second is Ruth Pickering, the two women killed in the fire. I don't understand." Wendy looked up at Sarah, like a student asking their teacher for help.

"Do you have a computer?"

"Well... yes. Back in my office."

Sarah followed Wendy back, looking through the doors of each office. The one at the end of the small hall still had a light on, and that was the one that Wendy went into to retrieve the pamphlets. It was a rather small office. Just big enough for the desk in it and the single guest chair that sat in front of the desk. If you were a guest, you wouldn't be able to slide it back farther, and you would need to scoot between it and the desk to sit. Marks scarred the wall behind it, where some hadn't realized that and slammed the chair backwards into it. On the far corner of the desk sat a docked laptop. Sarah sat down in the chair and attempted to roll the chair closer, but it didn't move. It couldn't, there were no wheels. She reached down and grabbed the seat and jerked it forward, causing the legs to chatter against the floor. Wendy stood on the other side of the desk, watching.

"You don't mind, do you?", Sarah asked.

Wendy said nothing to stop Sarah as she pulled up the web browser and went to the local news site. In a few clicks she found the story which had Lauren's picture under the headline. Sarah turned the laptop toward Wendy and held the pamphlet up next to it.

"Oh, my god," gasped Wendy. She stumbled back into the guest chair, sending it into the wall behind her.

9

Sarah reemerged from the office, leaving Wendy standing in the office doorway looking back out at them like she had seen a ghost, or had been told of a one. Sarah had told her what she planned to, needed to do. After seeing Ruth's picture, Sarah was convinced this was a case of mistaken identity, of the paranormal kind. It is well known that spirits can latch hold of places that are familiar to them, that is why they typically stay around, or what others call haunt, their homes or other buildings that hold a particular importance to them. The same holds true for people. No one knows for sure if emotions and memories remain once you die. Sarah hopes they do. She couldn't imagine not remembering her family after she is gone. Something about that sounds more like hell than heaven. There were cases after cases of a spirit interacting with someone that bore a similarity with someone they knew when they were alive. Sometimes the encounter was nothing more than lingering close to the person, causing them to get the "creeps" or feel the occasional chill, and others were of the more violent type. In those cases, whether they intended to do harm was not known. It could be as simple as just being the only way they knew how to reach the person from the other side. It didn't matter, Sarah dealt with them the same way.

When Sarah explained to Wendy what she needed to do, the woman sat there and stared at her in disbelief. A common expression when Sarah tried to explain such things to someone outside of their "special order". As Sarah kept explaining the "what and why", Wendy's arm rose. Not in a deliberate move, but more subconscious. The keys dangled from her hand. Sarah said, "Thank you," when she took them.

"What now?", Edward asked.

"I have no doubt the dark spirit we felt is the man behind the murders of the two women, and he attacked Lauren because she reminded him of Ruth. I need to remove him from the situation, permanently, or he will attack the next woman that walks through here that looks like her. It's not like a dog going nuts when it hears the doorbell, you can train them out of that behavior. With a spirit you have to remove them," explained Sarah as she led the parade back up two flights of stairs to the metal door. She turned the key and opened the door. The smell of freshly burnt wood and flesh wafted down the stairs and past her. She didn't need to wonder if any of the others could smell it, she already knew it was just her. Just like nobody else could see the last billows of smoke dancing around the light that hung over the stairs.

Leaving the others behind. Sarah and Sister Mary Theresa ascended the stairs for the second time. From behind them Father Lucian asked, "Did you sense the dark spirit when you were up there?"

"No," she said, stepping up another tread on the staircase.

"Do you need any help locating him?", he asked.

She paused on the next step to the top and turned around, "No, I have his room number." Sarah turned and stepped up on the landing and disappeared around the corner. Sister Mary Teresa followed her.

It was true, Sarah had his room number, or what she hoped was the room number. Wendy had told her that Mr. Baskin used room thirteen for his all-night poker games, and for his extracurricular activity. It would make sense that he would be there. As she walked down the hall, she passed room seventeen and felt Bette again, just like before. The room on the other side of the hall pulled at her, it was room sixteen. Sarah had every intention of continuing down to room thirteen to confront and deal with Mr. Baskin, but found she couldn't. Every time she attempted to step past room sixteen, something stopped her. It wasn't some spectacular paranormal force that trapped her feet to the floor. It wasn't a demonic presence putting up a spiritual barrier that she couldn't cross. No, it was something much simpler than that. It was her own curiosity. She wanted to go in and see, meet Ruth Pickering, so she did.

The door to room sixteen was not locked, and it opened easily. Like the room across the hall, it was trapped in time with the same mustard yellow and green decor. Sitting on the made bed, with it's mustard colored comforter, was a flickering Ruth Pickering. She was dressed in a periwinkle blue dress with matching buttons running up the center, matching shoes and hat, and white gloves. Two small brown suitcases sat next to her feet on the floor, all packed. Her striking blue eyes looked at Sarah as she walked through the door.

"Morning Sister, are you here to help me with my bags?", Ruth asked. She tugged at the hem of her dress, pulling out any wrinkles.

Sarah pondered that question before giving an answer. She gave every appearance of being all packed up and ready to check out. Perhaps that is how she was when the fire broke out, and she was now stuck there for all of eternity. Sarah knew that was something she could help with, "In a way, yes, I am."

"Good. That man down the hall has been making a commotion with the woman across the way all morning. I have to admit, some of what I have heard makes the thought of walking out into the hallway alone uncomfortable."

"Do you know the man?", Sarah asked.

"Oh, no. I have never seen him in all my life. I can tell you, he seems to have a temper and a mouth on him. All the swearing and pounding on the door." Ruth pursed her lips together as if the thought of what she had heard was sour to taste.

"So, they have been fighting?"

"All morning, and I am not talking about what most people would consider morning. I mean, from the time the clock rolled over past midnight." A single finger wagged at Sarah as Ruth spoke. Sarah could tell she had had enough, but was also concerned for her own safety.

"Could you tell what about?", asked Sarah, wondering if one of the reasons Ruth may have felt concerned for her own safety was because she had heard something she shouldn't.

"This and that. Mostly sounds like a lover's quarrel, even though there was nothing that sounded loving about it. It would seem she had a change of heart and he didn't agree, if you know what I mean. Some topics should be discussed behind closed doors, if you ask me."

"I completely understand," Sarah said.

"Good. Let me grab this one, and you can grab the other and I can get out of here before they start the noontime show," Ruth said and then bent down to grab the smaller of the two brown leather suitcases.

"Tell you what," Sarah started. "Why don't you just stay sitting right there for a few minutes. I want to go down and talk with him to make sure we won't have any more trouble from him, and then I will be right back to get you. Is that okay?"

Ruth let go of the case with a little thud. She sat back on the bed, her shoulders were no longer the straight back and proper posture they had been, they had a bit of a slump to them. Her hands joined one another on her lap, they were in constant motion, ringing each other out. "I do have places to go," her voice dripped of the same level of disdain her body showed.

"I promise. It won't be long. I feel it is something I need to do for everyone's safety," explained Sarah. "Is that all right?"

Ruth looked away from Sarah as she considered it. She looked back, but not at Sarah, around Sarah. Everywhere but her eyes. "I guess so," she said, rather tersely.

10

Sarah left room sixteen and headed down the hall for her next destination, room thirteen, and the man the ghost stories referred to as Mr. X. She felt his presence as soon as she passed the door for room fifteen. The sensation overwhelmed any residual tingling she'd had from Bette or Ruth. It was a different feeling altogether. The tingling and pricks on the back of her neck were there, and the hairs on her arms were standing up, but that was all normal. There was a weight, a heavy weight she felt pushing down on her, and an overwhelming claustrophobic feeling that made her want to duck below a low ceiling, even though the ceiling was still four feet above her head.

The closer she walked, the heavier the weight, and the closer the walls and ceiling became. A heat radiated toward Sarah, and she prepared herself for another wave of fire to rush past her, engulfing the entire floor like before. Such displays would intimidate most, but Sarah had seen this many times before. After the first wave hits her and she realizes they, and any pain she felt, were not real, she just ignored them.

The heat and weight were oppressive when she reached the door. As she reached for the knob, she wondered if both were meant for her. Was whatever behind the door aware of her? It was possible, since both Ruth and Bette were. This could also just be a normal state for anyone that approached. She looked behind her at sister Mary Theresa, who was doing her duty, showing no signs of any discomfort or effect. Sarah knew the dedication of her sisters, and considered that she might not give off any outward indications, so she asked, "Stai bene?"

Sister Mary Theresa nodded.

"Senti calore?", Sarah asked again, to be sure.

This time Sister Mary Theresa looked up from her prayer, and paused for just a second to say, "Nessuna sorella."

"Okay," and Sarah turned the knob.

There was no great fire inside, just another room like the others. Same colors and interior decorating theme. Same furniture. A man's sports coat lay on the bed and a pair of black leather shoes sat on the floor beside the bed. The man that wore them was nowhere to be found. The sound of water running in the bathroom, and steam coming out past the partially closed door, hinted at where he was. A valve squeaked, and the water shut off. Sarah heard the sound of metal scraping on metal.

It sent shivers through her body. That sound, and the sound of fingernails on a chalkboard, had always been the two that made her skin crawl. If someone ever really wanted to torture her, all they would need to do is trap her in a room with that sound. This particular sound was one she recognized. It was why she'd swapped out the shower curtain rings in her bathroom with plastic ones.

The bathroom door opened and a middle-aged man with dark hair walked out. A towel was wrapped around him from the waist down. His hands worked another towel through his hair and over his face. To say he looked surprised after he lowered the towel and saw Sarah standing there was inaccurate. He appeared shocked, and stammered for a few moments, just looking at her as he took a step here, and another there. He appeared to gather himself and righted his posture. It even appeared to Sarah that he sucked in his stomach and puffed out his chest. Not that it did much. The man's physique was far from being considered out of shape. Broad shoulders, a nice well-defined chest that led to a tight and rippled abdomen that trapped a few remaining drops of water from his shower. He threw the towel over the arm of a nearby chair.

"Going to church on Sundays isn't enough? You guys are now offering a delivery service, is that it, Sister?", his tone cut through the room and cut through Sarah.

"No, sir. I am here to help," she said, trying to keep it simple. She still felt all the normal sensations, as well as the heat and weight, but couldn't tell if this was just a spirit or if there was a demonic presence here. There was no need to tip her hand and have the situation turn messy, yet.

"Help," he chuckled. "The help I need is something you can't provide." He walked over and retrieved a white undershirt and pair of boxers from an overnight case sitting on the maple wood bureau. His gaze locked on her.

"I hear there were some problems here this morning, and I want to smooth things out for all involved."

He chuckled again. But this had an acidic tone to it, and the weight of the air around Sarah increased, bearing down on every inch of her.

"You want to smooth things out? What exactly do you want to smooth out, Sister?" He leered at her and threw the undershirt in a ball of fabric onto the bed. She hadn't noticed how harsh his eyes looked before. She had to assume they were brown, but the color was so dark they looked pitch black, like pieces of coal swimming in a sea of white. "You are kind of cute, for a nun. Maybe you could smooth something out," he said and flashed a cigarette-stained smile at her and dropped the towel.

Without even a quiver of shock in her voice, Sarah responded, "Not in that way." She stepped forward, her hands together in front of her. "I feel you are someplace you shouldn't be, and your presence here is hurting people. I can help you find your way home." Sarah decided to go ahead and pitch it out there and see if he would take the easy way.

"I am right where I need to be. What is it, Sister? Have you never seen a naked man before? I know you guys take some kind of oath," he walked toward her, being sure to exaggerate the movements of his pelvis as if he was putting on a show for her. "Vow, that is what you call it," he corrected as he snapped his left hand.

Sarah asked, "Sir, why are you here?"

"I think you know. Of course, my stay would be better if she hadn't found her conscience and turned me down." He jerked to a stop and looked at the wall to his right before jerking his head around toward Sarah. "I think I finally figured out what your deal is, and why you are here. This is all your fault."

The air pushed down on her with a crushing force. Sarah's knees struggled to support her. The heat that was there now pulsed hotter and hotter.

"This is your fault. You talked to her and gave her some kind of moral dilemma. I don't give a shit about your morals," he exploded, and threw both hands into the air. Then he lunged for his overnight case and threw it against the wall. Both hands grasped his face. He glared at her through his fingers before one finger shot forward toward her, "What is it with you people? You and that nosy bitty down the hall. You think you are better than everyone and can sit in judgment. I know I heard her whisper, judging me. Each time she cracked open the door to see me and Bette talking in the hall. What, were you in the room with her, or the next room?" Distraught, he ran around the room, shoving chairs and tables over. His clothes were strewn all over the floor, pieces hung from the lamp, casting an eerie dark shadow on the wall behind him. It appeared to grow as the heat intensified. "I have worked too hard for what I have. I won't let you ruin this for me."

11

The man ran to his case that now sat at the base of the wall next to the nightstand. Its contents scattered along the floor. He picked up an aluminum bottle and ran toward Sarah. She jumped out of the way, slipped, and fell to the floor. His naked body ran past her, and through Sister Mary Theresa who stood in the doorway. The dark shadow that was on the wall followed behind him, along the floor and out.

Sarah rushed to her feet and followed. A very terse, "move" escaped her mouth as she approached her escort, who was unaware of what was happening around her. When she got to the hallway, she spotted him standing at the edge of the stairs, pouring the liquid on the carpet. He continued down the hall, past both rooms seventeen and sixteen. Sarah's nose burned and eyes watered. There was no mistaking the pungent odor of the fluid. He continued pouring the fluid and slammed Sarah against the wall as he passed by, continuing the line down the hall. It extended from the stairs halfway down the hall, just past his own room, which he ducked inside. Before Sarah reached the door, he was back out in the hallway with a chrome-plated lighter. He had already struck the flick to produce a flame. He stood there appreciating the glow which cast his facial features into an evil light.

"There is no reason to do this," Sarah said.

"That is where you are wrong," he sniped back. "There is every reason to do this. You, that busy body down the hall, and the tramp I brought with me, won't destroy me."

"You have already been destroyed. It is time to stop this and free yourself. Stop tormenting yourself and others," Sarah pleaded. The dark shadow left him for a moment and smacked into Sarah. She crashed into the wall. Its weight held her there and pushed harder until the plaster behind her cracked. She heard and felt the crack behind her. A shot of pain exploded from her ribs and caused her to wonder if one of the pops she'd heard was something inside her giving way. She screamed, and the force clamped down harder, pushing what air remained from her lungs. Each gasp for air only brought in fumes that burned her lungs.

"Stop. I won't let you tear apart everything I am," he declared and dropped the lighter onto the carpet. The line of fluid exploded in a blue wave that progressed from one end to another, before spreading out along the floor. He ran, still naked, into room seventeen. The shadow released its hold on her and followed the man. Sarah, feeling bruised from head to toe, rushed in after them. Through the bedroom and into the bathroom, where Sarah found the man with his hands around Bette's throat, forcing her under the water in the tub. She fought with all she had. Each time her head breached above the water, a scream escaped and filled the room.

Sarah went to intervene, but was too late. She reached to pull him away, but he turned toward her and grabbed her around the throat. Sarah kicked, pushing him away long enough to allow her to crawl to her feet. He caught her ankle before she reached the hall and slammed back to the floor. His touch produced a pain unlike any she had felt before. Another strategically placed kick to his forehead freed her again. His touch blackened her skin with soot.

Sarah pulled her way into the hall, but again, he was on her and pulled her back. He climbed on top of her, adding to the oppressive weight her body felt. Both hands grabbed her throat and wrenched back and forth, increasing pressure with each twist. Her breath was being ripped from her as her outsides were being burnt. Over and over, he repeated, "You won't take everything from me." The flames spread up the walls around her, to the ceiling above. To her right, she heard Ruth screaming as the fire ravaged her room.

"You are not a bad person. You just made a mistake. God will forgive you," Sarah croaked out in between gasps for breath. Smoke filled her lungs. She needed to cough. A task his hands wouldn't allow.

He retorted with a sinister smile, "I don't care about your God, Sister." The dark shadow grew over him. It could have been columns of black smoke, but she felt the evil grow.

"His glory will accept you into his kingdom for life ever after," she mumbled, in between two hacks to expel the smoke that invaded her airway.

He flickered and disappeared for a moment before reappearing. The crucifix around her neck began to glow. The light hit him in the face, and he leapt off of Sarah. Sarah pulled herself against the opposite wall. Every breath a struggle. She reached for the crucifix and basked in its warmth and comfort. On her knees, she crawled over halfway and faced him.

"He does not judge, for we are made in his image. Our flaws are his flaws. Whatever mistakes you made in this life won't cost you anything in the afterlife. Accept his truth and light in your heart, and you will join him." She used the crucifix to outline a cross in the air in front of him. A blast of heat and smoke shoved her back against the wall. Her head whipped backward, cracking the plaster. Behind him was the dark shadow again. It stretched up the wall and across the ceiling.

"This is not your vessel," she yelled. The shadow continued to creep toward her. Again, she directed her attention to the man, "Accept him into your heart and cast out any ill agents that whisper mis-truths and falsehoods into your ear. There is only one Lord, one Savior. Accept him and enjoy peace and love in the afterlife."

The man looked at her, eyes clear, full of fear. He appeared to attempt to mouth "How?" The shadow receded across the ceiling in a flash and entered him. The clarity she saw in his eyes was gone. The pits of darkness were back, and they gazed upon her with all the ill will in the world. Then he leapt at her. It wasn't a move, a leap, or a jump. A force launched his body at her.

Her mind said, "The hard way." She stood up and met it with a punch, sending it sprawling down the hall. It came at her again, and she dodged its attempt, landing in an ocean of flames that didn't burn her. The only one that had been burnt was the man. Sarah had contacted his chest with the crucifix as it flew over her. The spot sizzled and blue smoke wafted up from the wound.

It continued to sizzle as it made another pass. Again, Sarah hit him with her crucifix. This time, his body crumpled into a mass on the floor. She had done more damage, but was not unscathed herself. It got a good swipe in that time, down the center of her back. The pain had her lying flat on the ground.

Sarah struggled to push up off the floor, but collapsed after each of the first several attempts, from the pain. Through her tears, she watched him as he attempted to get to his feet. Finally she powered through the pain, making it to her knees. Then, one leg at a time, she made it to her feet and walked toward him. His body was twitching and contorted in unnatural ways. His chest was flat on the ground, but his face looked straight up at hers. He growled at her from deep inside his chest, while his mouth said, "I accept him."

"If only it were that easy now," she said as she knelt down next to him. "You accepted evil into your heart, and I must cleanse you."

Sarah placed the crucifix on his forehead. He writhed at its contact. The growl deep inside grew, vibrating the floor. "I cast you out, agent of evil, unclean spirit. Leave this vessel, for it is not yours." A blue flame exploded from the spot the crucifix touched and ran down the length of his body, filling the hallway with blue smoke. His body turned to ash and then faded away, as did the flames from the fire he'd started.

Sarah stood up from where she knelt. The pain in her back was gone, as were the soot smudges from where he had touched her. She had dismissed him, so he wouldn't bother anyone again, but she didn't feel her work was done yet, and went into room seventeen, into the bathroom. Bette laid there in the tub, motionless. Sarah knelt beside her and gave her her last rites. Her presence flickered once, slowly, and then faded away. There was one more task for Sarah to do.

Ruth Pickering sat on the bed right where Sarah had left her earlier. "Are you ready to go?"

"Well, I didn't pack up for the health of it."

Sarah sat next to her and took her hand. "You were trapped here through no fault of your own. You are one of our Lord and Savior's creatures and are now allowed to return to him. Do you accept him into your heart?"

"Yes. I do and always have."

12

"I will say, looking back at all that now, it was rather intense. It wasn't my only time dealing with multiple spirits, but this was the first time I had to deal with such raw emotion that spilled out of them. It was when I realized they weren't that different than we are. Of course, that is a hotly contested point."

"What do you mean?", Ralph asked.

"Well, Father Lucian told me until his death, that he believed I was supplanting the emotions I would have felt in those situations onto them. I tended to believe he felt that way because he had never felt that from any of his experiences. Of course, there is nothing scientific about any of this. He could be right," she said, holding up a hand, palm pointed up to the ceiling. "Or I could be," she smirked and raised the other hand. "No one will ever know. It is all perspective. See, much of life is. Very little is black or white. It is mostly shades of gray. It's we who paint the lines."

"Yes, we do, don't we," Ralph said smiling. "Did dismissing, as you have called it before, stop the attacks?"

"I presume so. There were only two known attacks. The actual crime in 1941, and the one against Lauren Middleton. Since our visit, there have been no other issues, or as far as I have heard. Which saddens me a little."

Ralph acted surprised at that answer. He leaned forward and probed, "Why is that? If you don't mind me asking."

"While I removed an entity that had given himself over to dark forces, I also allowed two innocent spirits to find peace. For that I am happy, but I also robbed the world of a good ghost story." A mischievous smile crossed her face.

"I see. They can still tell the story though."

"They can, and I am sure they do. There just aren't any natural, or unnatural, bumps in the night to give those that go looking that little jolt."

The entire room chuckled at that reply. Kenneth stood up from behind the camera to look on the group with his own eyes.

"You took away a ghost story and solved one," he stopped and then corrected himself, "two crimes. I am sure the local law enforcement agencies were happy about that."

"Well, in a way. It conflicted them. They had the answers to both the 1941 murders and the current one, but that presented another and much larger problem.

How to report and document both. They very well couldn't document that a ghost killed Lauren Middleton, now could they?"

"So how did they handle it?"

"The case is still a cold case, just in a different cabinet, so no one will ever go looking again. The same with the 1941 murders of Bette Richeson and Ruth Pickering."

"But they had a name, right?", Ralph questioned. His pad emerged with his handy pencil. Both sat at the ready to make a note.

"Nope. Well, yes, they had a name, or Detective Burrows did, and that is as far as it went. See, I made that man a promise. When he looked up at me and told me he accepted God, I promised to not tear him down."

"So you won't tell us the name?"

"Nope, but I will tell you who it wasn't. It wasn't Marjorie Rawlings. I am sure you figured that out on your own. It also wasn't her husband, Norton Baskin. Whether or not any of the rumors, or any part of the story about them is true, I don't know. He was an unrelated man, a married man, an important man, who was at their hotel for an encounter with his girlfriend. A woman who had a moment of conscience and thought better of their relationship, and refused him. Hearing the word "No", was not something he was used to."

Have you read the whole Miller's Crossing series?

Miller's Crossing Book 1 – The Ghosts of Miller's Crossing

Amazon US
Amazon UK

Ghosts and demons openly wander around the small town of Miller's Crossing. Over 250 years ago, the Vatican assigned a family to be this town's "keeper" to protect the realm of the living from their "visitors". There is just one problem. Edward Meyer doesn't know that is his family, yet.

Tragedy struck Edward twice. The first robbed him of his childhood and the truth behind who and what he is. The second, cost him his wife, sending him back to Miller's Crossing to start over with his two children.

What he finds when he returns is anything but what he expected. He is thrust into a world that is shocking and mysterious, while also answering and great many questions. With the help of two old friends, he rediscovers who and what he is, but he also discovers another truth, a dark truth. The truth behind the very tragedy that took so much from him. Edward faces a choice. Stay, and take his place in what destiny had planned for him,or run, leaving it and his family's legacy behind.

Miller's Crossing Book 2 – The Demon of Miller's Crossing

Amazon US
Amazon UK

The people of Miller's Crossing believed the worst of the "Dark Period" they had suffered through was behind them, and life had returned to normal. Or, as normal as life can be in a place where it is normal to see ghosts walking around. What they didn't know was the evil entity that tormented them was merely lying in wait.

After a period of thirty dark years, Miller's Crossing had now enjoyed eight years of peace and calm, allowing the scars of the past to heal. What no one realizes is under the surface the evil entity that caused their pain and suffering is just waiting to rip those wounds open again. Its instrument for destruction will be an unexpected, familiar, and powerful force in the community.

Miller's Crossing Book 3 – The Exorcism of Miller's Crossing – Available Fall 2020

Amazon US
Amazon UK

The "Dark Period" the people of Miller's Crossing suffered through before was nothing compared to life as a hostage to a malevolent demon that is after revenge. Worst of all, those assigned to protect them from such evils are not only helpless, but they are tools in the creatures plan. Extreme measures will be needed, but at what cost.

The rest of the "keepers" from the remaining 6 paranormal places in the world are called in to help free the people of Miller's Crossing from a demon that has exacted its revenge on the very family assigned to protect them. Action must be taken to avoid losing the town, and allowing the world of the dead to roam free to take over the dominion of the living. This demon took Edward's parents from him while he was a child. What will it take now?

Miller's Crossing - Prequel – The Origins of Miller's Crossing

Amazon US
Amazon UK

There are six known places in the world that are more "paranormal" than anywhere else. The Vatican has taken care to assign "sensitives" and "keepers" to each of those to protect the realm of the living from the realm of the dead. With the colonization of the New World, a seventh location has been found, and time for a new recruit.

William Miller is a simple farmer in the 18th century coastal town of St. Margaret's Hope Scotland. His life is ordinary and mundane, mostly. He does possess one unique skill. He sees ghosts.

A chance discovery of his special ability exposes him to an organization that needs people like him. An offer is made, he can stay an ordinary farmer, or come to the Vatican for training to join a league of "sensitives" and "keepers" to watch over and care for the areas where the realm of the living and the dead interaction. Will he turn it down, or will he accept and prove he has what it takes to become one of the true legends of their order? It is a decision that can't be made lightly, as there is a cost to pay for generations to come.

ALSO BY DAVID CLARK

Want more frights?

Ghost Storm – Available Now

Amazon US

Amazon UK

There is nothing natural about this hurricane. An evil shaman unleashes a super-storm powered by an ancient Amazon spirit to enslave to humanity. Can one man realize what is important in time to protect his family from this danger?

Successful attorney Jim Preston hates living in his late father's shadow. Eager to leave his stress behind and validate his hard work, he takes his family on a lavish Florida vacation. But his plan turns to dust when a malicious shaman summons a hurricane of soul-stealing spirits.

Though his skeptical lawyer mind disbelieves at first, Jim can't ignore the warnings when the violent wraiths forge a path of destruction. But after numerous unsuccessful escape attempts, his only hope of protecting his wife and children is to confront an ancient demonic force head-on... or become its prisoner.

Can Jim prove he's worth more than a fancy house or car and stop a brutal spectral horde from killing everything he holds dear?

Have you read them all?

Game Master Series

Book One - Game Master – Game On

This fast-paced adrenaline filled series follows Robert Deluiz and his friends behind the veil of 1's and 0's and into the underbelly of the online universe where they are trapped as pawns in a sadistic game show for their very lives. Lose a challenge, and you die a horrible death to the cheers and profit of the viewers. Win them all, and you are changed forever.

Can Robert out play, outsmart, and outlast his friends to survive and be crowned Game Master?

Buy book one, Game Master: Game On and see if you have what it takes to be the Game Master.

Available now on Amazon and Kindle Unlimited

Book Two - Game Master – Playing for Keeps

The fast-paced horror for Robert and his new wife, Amy, continue. They think they have the game mastered when new players enter with their own set of rules, and they have no intention of playing fair. Motivated by anger and money, the root of all evil, these individuals devise a plan a for the Robert and his friends to repay them. The price... is their lives.

Game Master Play On is a fast-paced sequel ripped from today's headlines. If you like thriller stories with a touch of realism and a stunning twist that goes back to the origins of the Game Master show itself, then you will love this entry in David Clark's dark web trilogy, Game Master.

Buy book two, Game Master: Playing for Keeps to find out if the SanSquad survives.

Available now on Amazon and Kindle Unlimited

Book Three - Game Master – Reboot

With one of their own in danger, Robert and Doug reach out to a few of the games earliest players to mount a rescue. During their efforts, Robert finds himself immersed in a Cold War battle to save their friend. Their adversary... an ex-KGB super spy, now turned arms dealer, who is considered one of the most dangerous men walking the planet. Will the skills Robert has learned playing the game help him in this real world raid? There is no trick CGI or trap doors here, the threats are all real.

Buy book three, Game Master: Reboot to read the thrilling conclusion of the Game Master series.

Available now on Amazon and Kindle Unlimited

Highway 666 Series

Book One – Highway 666

A collection of four tales straight from the depths of hell itself. These four tales will take you on a high-speed chase down Highway 666, rip your heart out, burn you in a hell, and then leave you feeling lonely and cold at the end.

Stories Include:

- Highway 666 - The fate of three teenagers hooked into a demonic ride-share.
- Till Death – A new spin on the wedding vows
- Demon Apocalypse - It is the end of days, but not how the Bible described it.
- Eternal Journey - A young girl is forever condemned to her last walk, her journey will never end

Available now on Amazon and Kindle Unlimited

Book Two – The Splurge

A collection of short stories that follows one family through a dysfunctional Holiday Season that makes the Griswold's look like a Norman Rockwell painting.

Stories included:

- Trick or Treat – The annual neighborhood Halloween decorating contest is taken a bit too far and elicits some unwilling volunteers.
- Family Dinner – When your immediate family abandons you on Thanksgiving, what do you do? Well, you dig down deep on the family tree.
- The Splurge – This is a "Purge" parody focused around the First Black Friday Sale.
- Christmas Eve Nightmare – The family finds more than a Yule log in the fireplace on Christmas Eve

Available now on Amazon and Kindle Unlimited

Cover designed by Eye Creation

David Clark
Visit my website at www.authordavidclark.com

Printed in the United States of America

First Printing: December 2020

Printed in Great Britain
by Amazon

75173398R00031